Come Find Me

Written by:
Ken Harvey

Illustration by:
Terry Crews

First Printing, 1997
ISBN 978-17326906-0-8

Amen & Amen Publishing
117 East Colorado Blvd.
Suite 600
Pasadena, CA 91105

www.comefindmebook.com

This book is dedicated to my wife Rebecca, my daughters, Naomi, Azriel, Tera, Wynfrey, my son, Isaiah, my granddaughter Miley and all future generations of the Crews Family. I love you all with all my heart.

Terry Crews

I would like to dedicate this book to my three boys, Nathaniel, (who passed away from SIDS) Anthony and Marcus, my wife Janice, the rock in our family and my mother and father from whom I learned parenting.

Ken Harvey

20 years ago, 1995 to be exact, Ken Harvey and I were teammates on the NFL's Washington Redskins. Ken came to me with a
brilliant idea of a book he wrote for his two very young sons, Anthony and Marcus. The book was to be a first time reader, and feature the boys
in an imaginative game of hide and seek. The idea itself at the time was groundbreaking. Two young African-American boys,
imagining themselves as pilots, conductors, captains, and race car drivers was awesome, and greater
still was the ideological notion that it was one person's responsibility to look out for the other, even if it were just a fun game.
The book he wrote, and I illustrated, was COME FIND ME.

Now the boys are grown men, Ken is a successful businessman and I am known all over the world as an actor, artist and activist.
The little boys featured in this book, both graduated college, and have masters degrees in their respective fields of study.
I believe their success began when their Dad wrote "Come Find Me" and they envisioned themselves as the adventurous
characters in this book.

I hope every little boy and girl on earth, from whatever country, background or race can see themselves as imaginative,
fun and loving as Anthony and Marcus, and most importantly, parents and kids have a wonderful time as they enjoy the experience
of reading this book together.

Terry Crews

The reason I wrote "Come Find Me" was one of my boys asked me a question about an entertainer who lightened his skin.
He explained he saw a contest on TV where if you won, you could be one of the characters, but he was saddened because there
were no brown characters, hence the question about skin lightening. As a father it pained my heart to see what my son was going through.
I wanted to write a book where both boys could see themselves, but any other kids could see themselves too.

Ken Harvey

Terry Crews

Marcus and Anthony Harvey

Ken Harvey

Anthony, come find me!

Where are you Marcus?

Are you on a boat?

Nope, not on a boat.

Are you on a train?

Nope, not on a train.

Are you in a tree?

Nope, not in a tree.

Are you on an airplane?

Nope, not in an airplane.

Are you on a bus?

Nope, not on a bus.

Are you in a car?

Nope, not in a car.

Oh, I give up. Where are you?

Silly, I am right behind you!

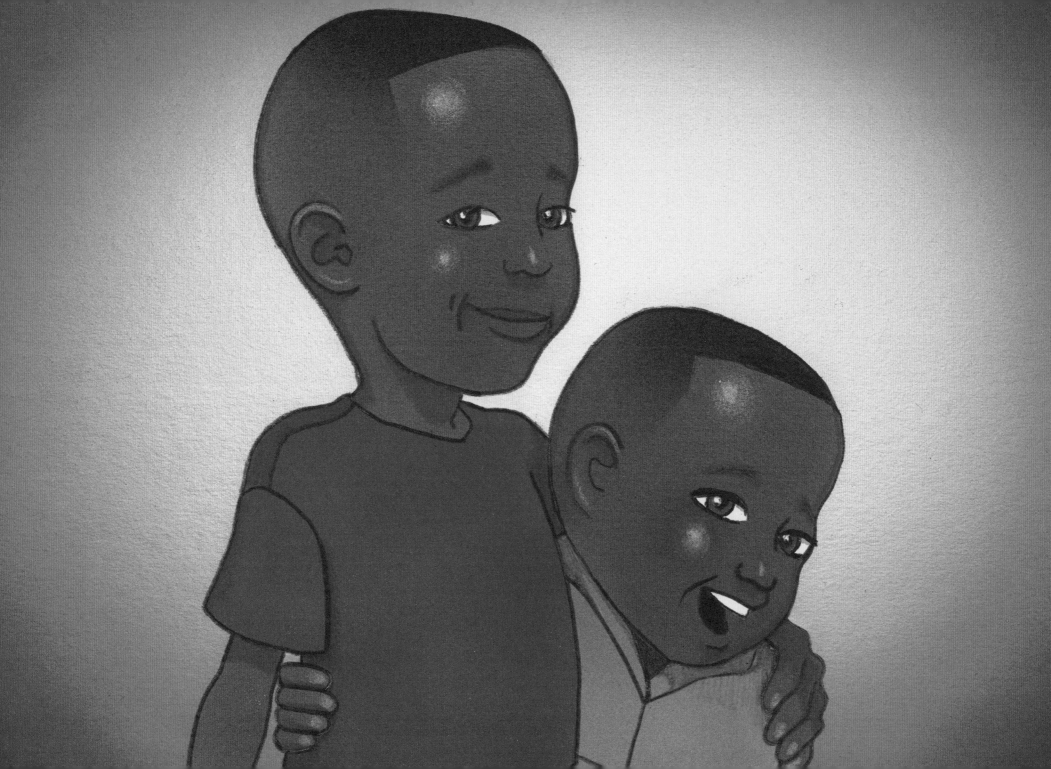